Through Moon and Stars and Night Skies

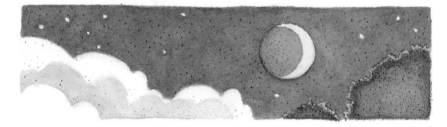

BY ANN TURNER

PICTURES BY JAMES GRAHAM HALE

A Charlotte Zolotow Book

An Imprint of HarperCollins*Publishers*

Also by Ann Turner

Heron Street

Through Moon and Stars and Night Skies
Text copyright © 1990 by Ann Turner
Illustrations copyright © 1990 by James Graham Hale

Library of Congress Cataloging-in-Publication Data
Turner, Ann Warren.
  Through moon and stars and night skies/by Ann Turner; pictures
by James Graham Hale. — 1st ed.
      p.   cm.
  "A Charlotte Zolotow book."
  Summary: A boy who came from far away to be adopted by a
couple in this country remembers how unfamiliar and frightening
some of the things were in his new home, before he accepted the
love to be found there.
  ISBN 0-06-026189-7 : $ ISBN 0-06-026190-0 (lib. bdg.) :
$
  [1. Adoption—Fiction.   2. Parent and child—Fiction.]   I. Hale,
James, ill.   II. Title.
PZ7.T8535The 1990
[E]—dc19   87-35044
                                                       CIP
                                                        AC

Printed in the U.S.A. All rights reserved.
Typography by Christine Kettner
      6   7   8   9   10

For Zane and Kara,
who always liked this one.

For
BEA
love,
Ann Turner
1996

Let me tell the story this time, Momma.
Let me tell how I came to you.
Momma said, Let's remember. Once
I was a picture you held in your hand.
Shhh, Momma. I will tell how I carried all your pictures
all the way to you.

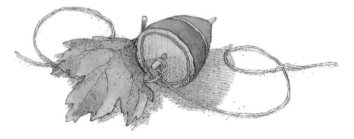

One was of my new poppa and momma.
Another was of your red dog, they told me.
There was a white house with a green tree out front.
Inside was a room waiting for me.
And a bed just for me.
On that bed was a teddy-bear quilt—waiting for me.

I needed a bed of my own.
I needed a poppa and momma of my own.

But I had to fly for a day and a night to get to you.
I was afraid—of flying, of the night,
of all the new things.

Someone took my hand.
I climbed the long steps to the plane.
It was bigger than ten houses.

A woman sat beside me all the way to you.
I flew through blue skies and clouds and sunlight.

I flew through night and moon and stars.

But I did not sleep. I was afraid.
Of the night rushing by.
Of the plane roaring.
Of all the new things.
I kept your picture in my hand all the way to you.

The earth rushed up below.
The plane bounced.
The woman took my hand and led me down the steps,
through a line, to a room with too many people.

But I looked and looked and saw you!
You both held out your arms to me.
The woman gave me to you, Momma.
We cried. Both of us.

I was still afraid. Of Poppa and you.
I was afraid of all the new things.

You took me home, Momma, sitting beside me.
You held my hand all the way.
But I did not sleep. I was afraid.
We stopped in front of the white house with a green tree.
I knew it was my house!

You hugged me and lifted me out of the car.
First we stopped by the green tree.
You put a leaf in my hand and smiled.
You took me inside.

The room was full of strange things.
It had dark corners.
You tried to put me down, but I yelled.
I did not want to be in that strange room.

Then I heard a bark!
The red dog ran up to me.
He jumped and licked my hand.
My new poppa pushed him down, but I did not cry.
I liked the red dog.

Momma, you smiled at me.
I was beginning to know your smile.

Poppa took me upstairs.
We sat in the rocking chair by the window.
I held your pictures in my hand.
Poppa pushed his feet against the floor.
We rocked back and forth, back and forth.
He fed me and held me close.
I looked into his eyes. They were dark and warm.
I was beginning to know his face.

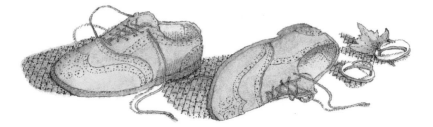

Momma, you held out the teddy-bear quilt.
I touched it.
It was just like the picture.
You lifted me into my new bed.
You tucked the quilt around me.
It was soft and warm. I knew that quilt.

Poppa kissed me on the forehead.
I knew his eyes now. I knew his face.
Momma, you sang a song like the wind
in the leaves of the green tree outside.

I closed my eyes.
I knew your voice now. I knew your smile.
I was not so afraid anymore.

I came to the white house with the green tree.
I saw the red dog.
I had you, Momma, and a new poppa.
You would watch over me.

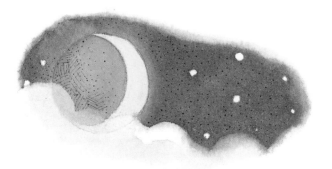

I went to sleep and dreamed of
moon and stars and night skies
and coming to a room where your arms were always
held out to me.